Where the Questions Go

Mehtab Hoque

Contents

Foreword

Some books ask to be read. Others wait quietly until the right reader arrives, not to simply pass the time, but to be changed by it. This is not a story that offers easy answers. It does not comfort with certainty or build walls with beliefs. Instead, it gently opens a door. On the other side, there is grief, love, wonder, doubt, silence, and something deeper still. Something that moves beneath our language like the current beneath ice.

This book began as a question. A question that might have been whispered in the dark when no one was listening. Why do we exist? Is there a purpose to our pain? What happens to the ones we love when they disappear from our lives? Is there a god, or only the longing for one? It did not grow into a novel in the traditional sense. It became more of a conversation between the seen and the unseen, the past and the future, the heart and the cosmos.

At its core, this is a story about a boy and a girl. About the weight of losing someone who felt like your anchor to the world. About walking forward when the ground no longer feels real. But more than that, it is a story of seeking. Of stepping into the most ancient and dangerous of questions with nothing but a journal and a broken heart. It is about how love survives not just time, but truth. How even in the most hollow places, a voice can still echo if someone is still listening.

I did not write this book to preach, to teach, or to convert. I wrote it because there are parts of us that exist beyond language and only stories know how to find them. This one found me in the stillness between thought and dream. It carried with it the feeling of hands reaching across dimensions, of questions written in ashes, of a name spoken softly after all the lights have gone out.

If you have ever stood beneath a sky too wide to understand, if you have ever wondered if there is more to this life than what we can touch, if you have loved and lost and still look for traces of them in strangers' faces or the shape of the clouds, then this book is yours.

Take your time with it. Let the silences speak. Let the questions sit with you for a while. Some of them may never be answered, but that does not make them any less sacred.

What you hold in your hands is not just a novel. It is a journey. And I am grateful you have chosen to walk it.

Mehtab Hoque

Preface

This book was not born from certainty. It was born from silence, from late nights where thoughts spun like constellations without names, from the ache of questions that refused to fade. I never set out to write a story about time travel, or grief, or faith. I only set out to understand what happens when everything we think we know is taken from us—and something still inside us refuses to stop searching.

The story you are about to read was never meant to be written. It arrived slowly, in fragments, like memories from another life. Sometimes through dreams. Sometimes through pain. And often through moments so quiet that they nearly went unnoticed. I carried it with me like a secret I wasn't ready to speak aloud. But some stories do not ask for permission to exist. They demand to be told because they belong not just to the one who writes them, but to everyone who has ever asked "why?"

Why do we lose the ones we love? Why does faith divide instead of unite? Why does truth change from mouth to mouth, from age to age? Is there a meaning to suffering, or is suffering the very thing that makes us human?

I did not write this to give answers. I wrote it to keep asking.

This story began with a character named Aldous. But it could have been anyone. Anyone who has carried loss like a second skin. Anyone who has stood in a room full of believers and wondered why their heart felt more empty than full. Anyone who has looked up at the stars and felt both infinite and unbearably small. Aldous is a mirror. He is a map through the ruins of belief. And at his side, always, is Leah—a presence that transcends space, time, and even death itself.

As you read, I ask only that you open yourself. Not just to the story, but to what lies between the lines. The things we do not say. The wounds we carry quietly. The longing for something beyond the veil of everyday life. Because this is not only a story about discovering the truth behind religion or the structure of the past. It is about what makes us keep going despite everything. It is about the soul's stubborn refusal to stop loving.

Writing this book changed me. Not by giving me clarity, but by allowing me to make peace with the unknown. If, by the time you reach the final page, you find yourself not with answers but with a heart that feels a little more open, a little more awake—then this story has done what it came here to do.

Thank you for holding it.

Mehtab Hoque

Acknowledgments

To write a book is to walk through a storm with a candle. There are moments when the flame nearly dies, when your own voice feels too small to carry the weight of the story. And yet, some lights never go out—because they are carried by others.

To everyone who has ever questioned the world they were handed, who has dared to doubt, who has loved deeply and lost painfully—you are the reason this story exists. Your questions echo in these pages. Your silence gave them room to grow.

To the voices of the philosophers, poets, and dreamers who came before—Camus, Kafka, Nietzsche, and all those who taught us that absurdity does not demand surrender but rebellion—I owe more than words can hold.

To my family and closest companions, thank you for understanding when I disappeared into this world. For your quiet support, your belief in something you couldn't see but trusted I was building. You gave me space to wander, and in that space, I found meaning.

To the readers—thank you. For choosing to walk beside Aldous. For feeling with him. For questioning with him. This book no longer belongs to me. It belongs to you, and to the still, burning part of you that refuses to stop seeking.

And lastly, to Leah. Not just a character, but a spirit born of memory, imagination, and love. She reminded me, again and again, that we never truly lose the ones we carry within us.

This book is a piece of my soul. Thank you for holding it with care.

Introduction

Why do we exist?

What lies beyond the veil of death, if anything at all? Is there a purpose to our suffering, or do we simply assign meaning to keep ourselves from unraveling? These are not questions with easy answers. They are the quiet storms that live in every thinking soul. For centuries, we have wrapped them in prayer and poetry, cloaked them in doctrine, or buried them beneath distraction. Yet still, they remain. They linger in silence, flickering behind the eyes of those brave or broken enough to ask. This is not a story that offers conclusions. It is a journey into the hollow space where faith and doubt collide. Where a single moment of loss can shake the spine of everything you believed. Where memory, belief, and time begin to blur. This book does not preach, and it does not condemn. It listens. It wonders. It aches. And most of all, it dares to imagine that there is more to reality than we have allowed ourselves to believe. If you have ever stared at the ceiling late at night and wondered if something is watching you, or if nothing ever was, this story is for you. If you have ever questioned the shape of morality, the roots of truth, or the systems that decide what we worship, then perhaps these pages will feel like returning to a question you forgot you were carrying. Here, love is not decoration. It is defiance. Here, death is not an ending. It is an invitation. And here, in this story, the search for meaning is not something to be solved. It is something to be lived.

CHAPTER ONE
The Silence After Leah

The world had gone quiet, but not in a peaceful way. It was the kind of silence that rang in your ears, the kind that made you feel like even your heartbeat was too loud. Aldous Manson sat on the steps of the old chapel, watching people he no longer recognized walk out of Leah's funeral. Their faces were damp, their hands folded, their mouths full of God. And all he could think was, *None of you really knew her.*

His hands were trembling. Not from the cold, though it was biting. He was trembling because everything in him was cracking, and it wasn't just because Leah was gone. It was what they said about her now that she was gone.

"God called her home," they whispered.
"She's with the angels."
"She's in a better place."

And Aldous wanted to scream, because none of them were there when Leah sobbed in his arms, said she didn't believe in any of that. Said she was tired of pretending for her family, for the church, for a God that never answered.

The last time she spoke to him—really spoke to him—was on that bench behind the science building, three days before she jumped into the river.

"I don't think anything's waiting for us, Aldous," she'd said. "I think we just end. Like a candle being blown out."

He remembered holding her hand, her fingers cold even then. He remembered saying, "Then let's burn as bright as we can."

But now she was gone, and the candle was out, and they were feeding him nonsense about paradise.

Inside the chapel, his father, Reverend Elias Manson, stood tall behind the pulpit. His voice filled the air, solemn and rehearsed. "Leah was a faithful child, though she struggled with doubt. We must trust in God's plan, mysterious though it may be."

Aldous stood up, the wooden steps creaking beneath him. He walked in, not because he wanted to, but because he couldn't stay outside any longer. The lies were louder out there.

His father noticed him immediately. His eyes narrowed.

Aldous sat in the back pew. He could feel the eyes of others shifting toward him. He hadn't spoken to most of these people in months. Some of them thought he was the reason Leah "strayed." The boy who asked too many questions. The one who challenged sermons with philosophy books and called Sunday school "indoctrination camp."

He didn't care what they thought. Not anymore.

What broke him wasn't their judgment. It was the photograph on the casket. Leah, laughing, caught mid-smile, her eyes full of fire. The girl they buried today was not the girl in the photo. That girl had been alive. She had hated hypocrisy, loved thunderstorms, believed in Aldous more than anything.

When the service ended, people gathered around Elias, praising the eulogy. Martha, Aldous's mother, kept glancing at him like she wanted to pull him away, but she didn't move. She knew better than to touch him when he was like this.

He walked up to the casket. Alone. He placed a small paper flower next to the photo. Leah used to fold them during detention. She said she liked the way something so fragile could be made by hand.

"Hey, Firefly," he whispered. "They're telling everyone you found peace. But I know you. You weren't looking for peace. You were looking for the truth."

His father's voice came from behind him. "It's time to let go, Aldous."

Aldous didn't turn around. "That's easy for you to say. You never saw her for who she really was."

Elias's voice dropped. "This is neither the time nor the place."

"You're right. That was three months ago, when you caught her with my books and told her she'd go to hell."

Elias gritted his teeth. "She needed guidance."

"She needed someone to listen."

He turned and walked out. No one followed him.

That night, he sat alone in his room. Leah's sweater still hung from the corner of his chair. He pressed it to his face, breathing in what little scent remained. He opened his journal, the one Leah had gifted him last winter.

On the first page she had written:
"Fill these pages with the questions they're too afraid to ask."

Aldous stared at the blank page.

He didn't know what to write. Not yet.

He lit a candle. Not because he believed it meant something. But because she used to say everything felt more honest in the glow of fire.

"I'm not letting this be your ending," he said out loud.

The next day, Aldous skipped school. He walked down to the riverbank where they'd found her. The wind carried the faint smell of pine and water. The current moved steadily, uncaring.

He sat by the edge for hours. At one point, a girl from school named Elsie walked past and paused.

"You okay?" she asked.

He didn't answer.

She sat next to him anyway.

"You know, Leah always talked about you. Said you were the only person who ever made her feel seen."

He glanced at her. "Then why did she leave?"

Elsie was quiet for a long time. Then she said, "Maybe because being seen wasn't enough. Not when the rest of the world wanted her invisible."

It was the first honest thing anyone had said to him in days.

Later, she asked, "Do you believe in heaven?"

"No," Aldous said. "I believe in pain. And fire. And a silence that never leaves."

She nodded slowly. "That's fair."

When she left, she didn't say goodbye.

That evening, Aldous went into the attic. He hadn't been up there in years. Dust clung to every surface, old bookshelves lined with forgotten theology and broken photo frames.

He found an old box of Leah's things. Inside was a notebook. Not her journal, but something else. Notes, ideas, bits of philosophy scribbled in margins. A thought repeated across several pages:
"Faith is comfort. Truth is war."

That night, Aldous didn't sleep.

Instead, he opened his laptop, pulled up files he hadn't touched in months, PDFs on ancient religions, conspiracy theories about organized faith, essays on atheism, clips from old debates, all the rabbit holes he and Leah had once gone down together.

He was going to find out where it all started—religion, belief, control. He was going to rip it open. Not to disprove God, but to understand why people needed Him so much they'd build walls and prisons and stories and gods to feel safe.

As the candle burned down to a nub, Aldous wrote in the journal.

"You said we were just candles waiting to go out. But I think we're sparks, flickering in the dark, desperate to light something before the wind takes us. I don't know what truth looks like yet, but I know yours is buried under a thousand lies. I'm going to find it. Even if I have to go back to where it all began."

CHAPTER TWO:

WHISPERS UNDER THE SKIN

"And those who were seen dancing were thought to be insane by those who could not hear the music."

— Friedrich Nietzsche

The rain didn't fall that night. It simply hung in the air, too heavy to descend, like the grief Aldous carried in his chest. He walked the streets with his hands buried in his pockets, the collar of his jacket upturned. The world around him seemed quieter now, like even the city had lowered its voice in mourning.

He passed the church he grew up in. Its lights were still on, windows glowing like eyes that had seen too much and said too little. The sign outside still read, *"God never makes mistakes."*

He stopped walking.

"Then where is she?" he whispered, not to anyone in particular. "Where the hell is she?"

His breath fogged the air. The street was empty, but his mind wasn't. Leah's voice still lived there, tucked between his thoughts like bookmarks he couldn't remove.

He remembered what she used to say whenever he doubted himself.

"You don't need to believe what they do, Aldous. You just need to believe that what you feel is real."

Now she was gone. And yet, somehow, she was still the only one who made sense.

A car drove by slowly. It was Reverend Elias—his father. Their eyes met for a moment through the rain-streaked window. No words. Just disappointment, unspoken and mutual.

Aldous kept walking.

He ended up at the old observatory on the hill. It had been abandoned for years, but the lock on the gate was still broken. Leah used to love it here. She said the stars looked more honest from this place.

He climbed to the roof, the city stretching below like a sleeping beast. The air was thinner here, sharper.

Aldous sat down, took out Leah's journal from inside his coat. The same pages he had nearly set on fire the night before. But he couldn't. Not yet.

One entry stood out, the ink smudged but still legible.

"I think heaven is just a story they tell people so they don't panic. But what if— just what if—it's something else? Not golden gates. Not angels. Maybe... just continuation. A different thread in the same fabric."

Aldous closed the journal.

A strange feeling passed through him—like being watched, but not by anything visible. It wasn't fear. It was something far colder. A presence without form. A whisper without breath.

Then, a voice, faint and clear.

"You're not supposed to be here yet."

Aldous stood up fast, heart pounding.

"Who said that?" he asked the night.

No answer. Just wind, and the occasional blink of a faraway star.

He turned—and saw her.

Leah. Or something that looked like her. A shimmer, a flicker. She stood at the edge of the roof, hair caught in the wind.

"You're not sleeping," she said, smiling faintly. "That's new."

Aldous stumbled back. "I'm going mad. That's what this is."

"Or maybe you're finally waking up," she said. "To what's always been under the surface."

He shook his head. "You're not real."

She shrugged. "Neither is most of what people believe. Doesn't stop them from killing for it."

Her tone shifted—familiar, sharp.

"You wanted proof, didn't you? Proof that all their sermons were scripted lies. That their god is a mirror they polished until they saw their own faces in it."

Aldous stepped closer. "What are you?"

She tilted her head.

"The question isn't *what* I am, Aldous. It's *why* you're seeing me. Why now."

Later that night, Aldous found himself back in his room, but it felt smaller now.

Too many thoughts for such a confined space.

He opened his laptop, typing into a search bar:

"Is religion man-made?"

"Historical origins of faith systems"

"Can consciousness survive death?"

The screen lit up with a thousand opinions. None of them answers.

That's when a message popped up on his screen. No sender. No subject. Just a sentence.

"If you want truth, look where they told you not to."

Attached was a video file. He hesitated. Clicked.

A black-and-white reel played: a documentary-style voice narrated over grainy images of early religious councils, political leaders cloaked in robes, men writing scrolls in candlelight. Their faces stern, calculated. Every word they wrote was a law, every silence a strategy.

"Religion was not born from faith," the voice said, *"but from fear. It was not written by the innocent, but by the powerful. It is the oldest performance art of control."*

Aldous stared at the screen, chills crawling up his spine. Not from fear, but recognition. Somewhere deep inside, he had always known.

A text appeared at the end of the video:

"Come find us. The ones who remember."

A set of coordinates followed.

The next morning, Aldous sat in front of his mother.

Her hands trembled over her tea. "You've changed," she said, eyes searching his face.

Aldous smiled faintly. "No. I'm just done pretending."

His father stormed in. "You've been talking nonsense again. What blasphemy are you spreading now?"

"Truth," Aldous said. "Something you fear more than hell."

The slap came, again, sharp and expected.

But this time, Aldous didn't flinch. He wiped the blood from his lip, looked his father dead in the eye.

"You preach about God's love, but you beat your children into silence. You lie to crowds every Sunday and call it scripture. Leah saw through you. And now, so do I."

His mother whispered, "Stop, please, just stop..."

But he didn't.

"I'm going to find out what this world really is," he said, voice steady. "What lies beneath all the gold-plated myths."

And with that, he left the house—maybe for good.

That night, on a rusted train heading toward the coordinates from the video, Aldous wrote in his journal:

"If truth is a war, then I'm a soldier without armor. But I've seen enough to know silence is its own kind of death. I'd rather burn in the truth than sleep in a lie."

Outside the window, the stars looked different now. Less distant. As if they were watching.

Waiting.

CHAPTER THREE

ASHES AND ECHOES

PART-I

The rain had stopped, but the smell of wet earth clung to Aldous's shoes as he walked along the empty street, Leah's journal pressed against his chest like a second heart. He hadn't slept. He didn't feel tired. Something had awakened in him—a restlessness that gnawed beneath his ribs, whispering that the world he had accepted so far was a lie, or at least, incomplete.

His fingers trembled as he opened her notebook again beneath the soft glow of the library's back porch light. Her writing was raw, sharp, angry at times, and painfully beautiful in others.

"I don't want heaven if it means pretending," one page read.
"What's the point of faith if it demands silence?" said another.
And the line that kept haunting him,

looping in his brain like a song with no melody:
"If God is love, why do I feel more seen when Aldous looks at me than when I kneel to pray?"

He remembered that look. The one she gave him when their hands brushed. When her eyes searched his like she was looking for permission to feel safe. And he gave it, silently, without knowing how important it was.

He sat on the stone steps, wind pushing his damp hair into his face. Around him, the town slept under layers of old guilt and clean church windows. Nothing looked broken on the surface, but Aldous knew how well this place hid its bruises. His family did it too.

Inside his jacket was the memory stick he'd found wedged between the pages of Leah's journal. It wasn't labeled. Just tucked there, like she wanted him to find it but couldn't say it out loud. He hadn't plugged it in yet. Maybe he was scared. Or maybe he wanted to hold onto the mystery a bit longer, afraid of what truths it might crack open

PART-II

He remembered how Leah used to talk to herself when she was nervous, humming under her breath like the world was a song she hadn't quite learned the words to. Now, in her absence, the silence between his breaths sounded louder than any melody she ever hummed. It had a shape, a texture—like absence could be something you touched. Something you swallowed.

The journal trembled slightly in his hand. Or maybe it was just him. The pages smelled faintly like lavender. She always used too much oil in her hair, and he had teased her for it. Now he missed it. Missed the scent of her defiance. Missed how she made ordinary things—like sitting in the sun or listening to thunderstorms—feel like rebellion.

"What is grief," he muttered to himself, "if not the world's most stubborn form of love?"

He opened the journal again, landing on a page he hadn't read yet. The handwriting was messier than usual. More frantic.

January 3rd
"Aldous doesn't see it yet. But he will. The thing we call God is just a cage with gold bars. It promises freedom but keeps our minds chained. I'm starting to think we're all just born into a story someone else wrote, and faith is the lie we're told to stop us from editing the ending."

He closed his eyes, biting the inside of his cheek.

A part of him wanted to scream at the sky. At God. At his father. But another part—the quieter, more dangerous part—just wanted answers. Not comfort. Not warmth. Not rituals. Truth.

The kind of truth that didn't wear a robe or speak from behind a pulpit.

It was nearly dawn when he made his way back home. The front door creaked like an old confession. His mother was asleep on the couch, Bible clutched to her chest like a shield. Her lips moved in sleep—silent prayers, maybe, or whispers to a God that Aldous no longer trusted.

He slipped past her and went to Leah's room. They hadn't touched it. The bed was still messy. The posters on the wall, the books stacked haphazardly, the faded glow-in-the-dark stars on her ceiling—still there. It felt like she'd only just stepped out.

He sat on her bed and plugged the USB into her old laptop.

The screen flickered to life.

One file.

"The Garden.mp4"

His stomach knotted.

He clicked it.

Static at first. Then Leah appeared, sitting on the floor in the same room he now sat in, wearing that oversized gray hoodie she used to steal from him.

Her eyes stared directly into the lens.

"If you're watching this," she said, voice a little shaky, "then I guess I'm gone."

She paused, looking down at her hands.

"They'll tell you I lost faith. That I let the devil in. But that's not true, Aldous. I just started asking the wrong questions. Or maybe the right ones."

Aldous leaned forward. His heart beat in his throat.

"I started reading. Ancient texts, forbidden ones, journals of mystics who were later called mad. I traced it all the way back—to the garden. The myth of Eden. The first lie."

Her voice was steadier now, like she'd rehearsed this a dozen times.

"Religion didn't begin with wonder. It began with control. With fear. They told us

Eve sinned by seeking knowledge, Aldous. But what if that was the beginning of truth, not the fall? What if her hunger wasn't a curse—but a rebellion?"

The screen went black.

Then a line of white text appeared:

"Go to the church basement. Under the altar. You'll know what to look for."

Aldous stared at the blank screen. His body felt numb. But his mind—his mind had never been clearer.

"They called her sinful," he whispered. "But maybe she was just awake."

He stood.

Walked to the window.

The sun was rising, painting the rooftops in gold.

"You're not gone," he said aloud, hand pressed to the glass. "You're just ahead of me."

In that moment, grief took a new shape—not a weight, but a compass. It no longer kept him still. It pointed somewhere.

Toward truth.

Toward the church.

Toward the altar.

PART - III

The air was colder than it should've been for a morning in late March. Not the chill of wind or winter, but the kind that comes from stepping into a place that has swallowed too many secrets.

Aldous stood outside the church doors.

The sun had risen just enough to cast long shadows down the brick steps. St. Mercy's Chapel loomed like it always had—tall and quiet, its bell tower empty, its windows glowing faintly with stained-glass saints and stories, none of which felt real anymore.

He had been here every Sunday since he was five.

He had knelt where he was told, sung what he was told, believed what he was told. Until Leah started whispering other things. Not loud. Not angry. Just... different.

"God doesn't love obedience," she once said while chewing on sunflower seeds. "He *needs* it. That's the difference."

He hadn't known what to say to that at the time. But it stuck. Like a thorn under his skin. Now it burned.

He pushed the doors open.

They moaned like something alive.

Inside, everything was as it always had been. Wooden pews. Red carpet. The pulpit, still draped in green for Lent. It smelled like incense and dust and silence.

He walked slowly, past the empty rows.

His footsteps echoed, soft but defiant.

The altar stood before him. Carved mahogany. Polished to shine like it had something to prove.

His fingers trembled as he reached out. Ran along the edge. Nothing obvious. But then, Leah would never have left him an obvious clue.

He knelt. Not in prayer. In purpose.

And there—beneath the altar cloth—he found a narrow latch.

It clicked.

The wood shifted with a groan and revealed a hidden trapdoor, its hinges rusted and dark. A narrow staircase twisted down into blackness.

He hesitated. Just once.

Then descended.

The basement smelled of old stone and damp rot. It wasn't part of the church anyone ever mentioned. His father had never spoken of it. And Aldous had asked too many questions in his life to think that was an accident.

There were candles down there.

Lit.

Not recently. But not long ago either.

His breath caught.

Books lined the walls. Not Bibles. Not hymnals. Manuscripts. Some handwritten. Some in languages he couldn't read. Others he recognized—fragments of the Gnostic Gospels, pieces of the Dead Sea Scrolls, heretical sermons burned out of history.

One book lay open on the table in the center.

Beside it, a notebook.

Leah's.

He opened it.

"This is where they hide the real faith," she'd written. "Not the kind that saves souls, but the kind that controls them. Here is where the rot begins. In the foundations. In the blood-soaked stones beneath the altar of obedience."

His hands shook as he flipped through.

Drawings of ancient temples. Marginalia linking sacrifice to obedience. Phrases underlined in red:

"Salvation demands surrender."
"Heaven is the price paid for silence."
"A god that cannot survive a question is no god at all."

Then a photograph.

Black and white. Faded.

Leah and Reverend Elias.

His father's hand on her shoulder.

But her eyes—they told another story.

Aldous staggered back.

His mind whirled.

His heart pounded.

He didn't know what was real anymore.
But he knew something had been broken.

Something Leah had found. Something dangerous enough to kill for.

He pressed his palm to the cold stone wall.

He needed to breathe. To think. To scream.

Instead, he whispered.

"You knew. You *knew*, Leah. And they punished you for it."

His voice cracked.

"I should've protected you."

Behind him, the shadows deepened. But he didn't turn.

In that moment, he wasn't afraid.

He was something else.

He was **awake**.

Back upstairs, the chapel was no longer silent.

His father stood at the doorway.

Clergy robes, eyes dark as a thunderhead.

"You shouldn't have gone down there," Elias said.

Aldous stared at him. At the man who raised him. At the liar.

"Neither should she."

"Leah was sick. Confused."

"No," Aldous said, stepping forward, voice sharp with grief, with fury, with love, "she was *brave*."

The silence stretched.

"You kislled her, didn't you?"

His father didn't flinch.

"Faith is not a toy, Aldous. It's a fire. Those who play with it get burned."

"Then I guess it's time I start playing."

He left the church that morning not as a boy lost in sorrow, but as something new. Something forged in fire and silence. Leah was gone—but her voice, her mind, her resistance lived in every word she left behind.

And now, it lived in him too.

He didn't know what he would find next.

Only that he would keep looking.

Because truth, he had learned, is not always found in answers.

Sometimes, it waits in the questions no one dares to ask.

Chapter Four:

The Silence Between the Stars

"Truth is not a destination. It is the ash left behind by the fire of all we thought we knew."

PART-I

He didn't go home that night.

Aldous wandered through the town like a ghost with a heartbeat, drifting down empty streets under the weight of a silence that was somehow louder than any sermon he had ever heard. The lamplight flickered above him, moths dancing in chaotic spirals around the glass like lost souls searching for something that would burn them clean.

He clutched Leah's journal close to his chest, the cover still stained with wax from the candlelit night before. Her words had etched themselves into him now—not just her thoughts, but the rhythm of her defiance, her skepticism, her fierce hunger to understand why the world insisted on binding itself to stories that never made sense.

He walked past the old diner where they used to sneak milkshakes after school. The red vinyl booths were empty. The jukebox, once filled with Leah's laughter and the low hum of The Cranberries, was now quiet.

He sat on the curb outside and opened her journal again, flipping to a page he hadn't dared read until now.

January 17th: The worst thing about this faith isn't that it's wrong. It's that no one wants to ask why. Why do bad things happen to the kind? Why is silence the only answer we get when we beg for mercy? They say God is in everything. Then He must be in the bruises too. Or maybe there's no one at all.

Aldous felt the burn in his chest. Not the pain of grief, but the kind of ache that comes when your world splits open and nothing underneath is what you were told.

He closed the book and looked up at the sky. The stars blinked overhead like cold, uncaring witnesses. Leah had once told him, half-laughing, that if God was real, He must be hiding behind Orion's Belt, too afraid to answer for the mess He left behind.

Tonight, Aldous believed her.

He met Harper again the next afternoon, near the abandoned rail tracks.

She was sitting on a rusted bench with a cigarette between her fingers and a paperback copy of Camus's *The Fall* on her lap. Her black boots were scuffed, and her eyeliner was smudged like she hadn't slept in days. She looked like someone who had spent years screaming into the void and finally taught herself how to whisper.

"Thought you'd be in church," she said without looking at him.

"I quit," Aldous replied, sitting beside her.

"Good. It was bad for your brain."

They sat in silence for a while, the wind combing through the trees. Harper flicked the ash off her cigarette and said, "You look like someone who just figured out God isn't home."

"I don't know if He was ever there."

She nodded like she understood that too well.

"I used to believe," she admitted, voice quieter now. "Really believed. I'd kneel beside my bed every night and whisper the same thing—'Please don't let him hurt me again.'"

Aldous turned to her. Her jaw clenched, but her eyes stayed soft, open.

"And then I'd wake up bruised anyway."

There was nothing poetic in that pain. Just the truth, raw and unfiltered.

He reached into his backpack and handed her Leah's journal.

"I think you should read this."

She looked at the book, then at him.

"Is it holy?"

"No," he said. "It's honest."

That night, Harper read under a flickering streetlight while Aldous sat beside her in silence. Occasionally, she'd laugh. Other times, her hand would cover her mouth as she swallowed grief that wasn't even hers.

"She was... brilliant," Harper said finally.

"She was more than they ever deserved," Aldous answered.

Days bled into weeks. Aldous started visiting the old town library more often, not for theology books like his father once forced him to study, but for philosophy, history, science. He read Descartes, Nietzsche, Simone Weil. Every answer led to a hundred more questions.

He found comfort not in certainty, but in doubt.

With Harper, he debated everything. Whether morality required God. Whether the soul was just a poetic way to explain neurons. Whether love itself was sacred or just evolutionary trickery.

Their arguments were loud, absurd, often fueled by cheap coffee and sleepless nights. But through it all, they laughed more than they cried. There was something redemptive about being seen, fully, in all your brokenness, and not turned away.

"I think," Harper said one night as they sat on the roof of the library, "that Leah wasn't trying to destroy faith. She was just asking if it had the right to survive."

Aldous smiled, tears blurring the stars above them.

"Maybe truth isn't the opposite of faith," he whispered. "Maybe it's what's left after faith burns away."

But not everyone was willing to let Aldous burn quietly.

Reverend Elias had grown colder, crueler. Rumors swirled around town—whispers of Aldous's "blasphemy," his rebellion, his influence over "impressionable girls." One Sunday, Aldous woke to find the front of their house painted with red letters:

LIAR. HERETIC. DEVIL'S SON.

His mother cried. His father said nothing.

Aldous stood there, eyes tracing the dripping paint, and thought, *Leah would've called it art.*

The war between belief and doubt had spilled into the open now, and Aldous knew there was no going back.

But he wasn't afraid anymore.

Not because he had answers.

But because he had the courage to live without them.

PART-II

That night, Aldous didn't sleep.

He sat cross-legged on the floor of his room, Leah's journal spread open in front of him, its spine worn from the nights he had read it like scripture. The moonlight spilled through the cracked blinds, casting thin, trembling lines across the ink-stained pages. Outside, the world was quiet—too quiet. Even the wind seemed to be holding its breath.

His mother hadn't knocked.

His father hadn't spoken.

But Aldous hadn't expected them to. Grief in their house was like wallpaper—faded, always there, always ignored. They mourned in silence, dressed it up in hymns and Sunday suits. But Aldous—he mourned with questions, with anger, with the unbearable ache of trying to remember the exact sound of Leah's laugh and failing.

His fingers paused over a passage in her journal, dated just weeks before she died:

"Sometimes I think the real hell is silence. Everyone around me praying with their eyes closed, while I'm the only one screaming with mine open."

He closed the book, pressing his palms against the cover like a prayer. Leah had seen it too—this hollowness in the rituals, the way belief could become a mask, a way to avoid facing the truth.

He stood and walked to his window. The stars were faint, but he could make out Orion above the rooftops. Leah used to say the stars weren't light, they were memories—echoes from a world that had already ended. "Looking at them is like reading the last page of a book written in fire," she once told him.

That was the first time she'd told him she didn't believe in heaven.

And now she was gone.

Yet somehow, she was more alive in these pages than any sermon had ever made her seem.

By morning, something had shifted inside him.

He packed a small bag—just a notebook, a half-dead phone, her journal, and a few clothes—and left the house. No note. No goodbye. Just the creak of the front door and the sound of his footsteps on the pavement.

He didn't know exactly where he was going. Only that he had to go. Somewhere beyond the script his father had written for him. Somewhere Leah might have gone if she'd been allowed to live without being watched, judged, silenced.

By noon, he was miles from the town.

The bus took him through places that felt unfamiliar in the best way. Gas stations that smelled like freedom. Old bookstores with windows so dusty they looked like forgotten dreams. Churches, too—always churches, standing like monuments to questions people were too afraid to ask.

He didn't stop at those.

But he did stop at an old café on the edge of a forgotten town, the kind of place where the clock didn't tick so much as breathe slowly.

A woman in her forties served him coffee. Her name was Miriam. Her eyes were kind but tired.

"You look like you've lost something," she said, handing him the cup.

He paused, then nodded. "I think I did."

She didn't press. She just sat across from him and lit a cigarette with hands that shook slightly.

"You know," she said, "I used to think faith meant never questioning. Now I think it means questioning so deeply, you scare yourself."

He looked at her, surprised. "You believe in God?"

She exhaled slowly. "I believe in the weight of a question. Some people call that God. Some call it madness. I call it being human."

They talked for hours.

About death.

About silence.

About the hollow echo that sometimes followed a prayer.

About love—how sometimes it feels more real after it's gone.

Miriam told him she'd lost a daughter once, too. Not to death, but to distance. "She stopped calling. Said I made her feel small. Maybe I did," she said, stirring her coffee slowly, like trying to find meaning in the swirl.

Aldous told her about Leah.

He didn't cry. Not then. But Miriam did.

And when he left, she pressed a small folded paper into his hand.

"Open it when you're too tired to keep going," she said. "Not before."

He walked for another day, then hitchhiked with an old man named Elias—not his father, but another Elias. This one wore suspenders and spoke like poetry was leaking from his bones.

"You've got the look of someone chasing ghosts," Elias said.

"Maybe," Aldous replied.

"They don't like being caught, you know. But sometimes, they lead you somewhere better than answers."

Aldous nodded, unsure why, but feeling it was true.

That night, he slept under the stars.

He read Leah's journal again.

One entry stuck out:

"If there is no god, it means we have to be better. If there is, and he lets this happen—then we still have to be better. Either way, the work is ours."

He lay there, staring at the sky, and whispered to the dark,

"I miss you."

No one answered.

But it didn't feel empty.

It felt like listening to the universe breathe.

In the morning, he woke to a question that burned hotter than any flame:

What if the afterlife isn't waiting for us—but already happening, right now, every time we choose love over fear, truth over comfort, freedom over obedience?

He didn't know.

But he wanted to find out.

And that was enough to keep going.

PART-III

The next town was smaller than the last. It looked like a place that had forgotten how to dream. Faded prayer flags hung between cracked buildings. The church had a crooked cross, and the school had no children playing. Aldous walked through it like someone drifting through memory— everything familiar in a way that felt wrong.

He found a bench near the edge of the cemetery and sat there for what could've been hours.

An old man approached him eventually, eyes like gray smoke, dragging a broom behind him like a tail of ash.

"You waiting for someone?" the man asked.

Aldous shook his head.

The old man leaned on his broom. "They all are, you know. Everyone buried here. Waiting for someone to remember their name. Waiting for someone to believe their story mattered."

"I don't believe in waiting," Aldous said.

"Then you've already outlived most of them."

He walked further, deeper into the countryside, until the roads stopped having names and the birds stopped singing. The air changed out there. It didn't feel like oxygen anymore—it felt like silence pressing down on the bones.

He stopped at an abandoned chapel. The wooden doors had caved in, vines choking the windows. Inside, dust settled like snow on rows of pews. A single stained glass window still clung to color—red and blue splinters bleeding across the floor.

Aldous stepped inside and sat where the pulpit once stood.

He imagined Leah there, standing on broken stone, her voice echoing off the cracked walls.

"What would you say now?" he asked the air.

And somehow, he could almost hear her.

"I'd say... you're still listening. And that means you haven't given up."

He smiled.

God, he missed her voice.

But it wasn't just grief anymore.

It was something more.

It was the ache of knowing she had lived in a world too small for her mind. A world that feared her questions. A world that wrapped lies in ritual and called it salvation.

And Aldous had been part of that world once.

He wasn't anymore.

That night, he opened the folded note Miriam had given him.

It read:

"When the world goes quiet, and your questions scream loudest, know this—truth is a mirror broken across a thousand souls. Each of us holds a piece. Some hide it. Some worship it. And some, like you, try to fit it back together."

Below it, a small line, hand-written in smaller ink:

"Find the others who bleed like you do."

He folded the note again and tucked it inside Leah's journal.

Then he slept. Not with peace, but with purpose.

Over the next few days, Aldous met others.

Not many.

But enough.

A girl in a bookstore who used poetry like a weapon. A boy who left seminary school after dreaming of fire and silence. A woman who believed God was real but cruel, and chose kindness anyway.

They didn't have the same stories, but they carried the same wounds.

And in each of them, Aldous saw a fragment of Leah.

Of himself.

There were nights he broke down.

Nights when the weight of the world felt like it would snap his ribs.

But he didn't run back.

He didn't pray for rescue.

He let the pain sit beside him.

He let it speak.

And it said things no sermon ever had.

Weeks passed.

Then one morning, as the sun spilled gold across the hills, Aldous found himself standing before a mirror in an old train station bathroom. His hair was longer. His face thinner. There were scars now, some on the skin, more beneath.

But there was something new in his eyes.

Not certainty.

Not faith.

But fire.

He scrawled a sentence on the wall with the last of his pen's ink:

"To ask is to live. To doubt is to love. To search is to be free."

And then he left.

Not toward a destination.

But forward.

Always forward.

PART-IV

The wind outside the station felt different. Not colder, just... aware. As if the world had been watching him scribble those words and now whispered them back through the rustling trees, through cracks in the old bricks, through the silence of things too tired to speak aloud.

Aldous didn't know where he was walking.

He had stopped needing destinations.

But his feet moved like they were chasing something ancient and wordless, like some compass buried in his blood had started twitching again.

He passed fields stitched together with fog and fences made of forgotten promises. The roads were bone-dry, splitting at strange angles, like veins on a dying leaf. Somewhere in the distance, a crow cawed once and nothing answered.

He crossed an old rail bridge, the kind that swayed under weight and smelled of iron and old storms. Beneath it, a dry creek bed split the land in two like a scar.

Halfway across, he stopped.

Because suddenly, it hit him.
The silence wasn't empty.

It was waiting.

And this time, it wasn't just memory or grief.

It was something else.
Something alive.

He knelt by the edge of the bridge and pulled Leah's journal from his coat. Flipping to a page marked with a dried flower, he stared at her handwriting like it was her face. His finger traced a line:

"Some places are wounds in the world. And some people were born to find them."

He shut the book and closed his eyes.

"Okay," he whispered. "I'm listening."

A soft breath of wind passed over the bridge. Nothing else. But it felt like the world had nodded.

That evening, he found shelter in a barn long abandoned by the living. The wood groaned in the night, but it didn't feel haunted. It felt held. Like the ghosts here knew how to make room.

He lit a candle stub and sat against the hay wall, knees pulled in, watching moths circle the dim flame.

Then, for the first time in days, he dreamed.

And in the dream---Leah was not dead.

She stood in a wide field, barefoot and laughing, the wind tangling her hair. She looked right at him and said,

"You never really lose someone. You just meet them again in different questions."

He woke up crying. Not loudly. Just a slow, silent leak from a soul trying to hold more than it was built for.

He whispered into the dark, "I don't want answers anymore. I just want to keep hearing you."

Something creaked in the barn rafters. A beam of moonlight cut through a gap in the boards and struck a stack of crates. He stood, walked over.

There, among rusted tools and broken plows, was a box. Ordinary. Plain wood. But nailed shut with odd, almost ceremonial care. Something about it made the hairs rise on his arms.

He didn't touch it that night.

Instead, he sat down next to it, lit another candle, and reread the letter from Miriam.

"Truth is a mirror broken across a thousand souls..."

He read it again.

And again.

Because the world wasn't just giving him metaphors anymore.

It was giving him clues.

The next morning, he broke the box open.

Inside was a machine.

Worn, strange, impossibly old and yet impossibly new.

Not a time machine in the cinematic sense.

No gears or glowing lights.

Just a black, polished device the size of a book, engraved with symbols that looked like a fusion of languages he'd never studied and dreams he'd never had.

Underneath it, folded neatly, was a sheet of instructions written in handwriting he recognized instantly.

Leah's.

He froze.

Heart roaring. Hands trembling.

He read the first line aloud, voice cracking like ice:

"If you're reading this... then you've finally started listening."

PART-V

Aldous stared at the machine in his lap, Leah's words breathing against the quiet morning.

"If you're reading this... then you've finally started listening."

It felt impossible—and yet, this whole journey had been a slow, unfolding impossibility. The grief, the strangers, the broken chapel, the mirror message, the dream, each piece like a breadcrumb from someone who shouldn't have been able to leave any.

And now this.

The device was cold. Too cold for wood or metal. Like it held a stillness deeper than time. The surface shimmered faintly in the light, symbols crawling softly beneath the black like breath under skin.

He kept reading.

"You'll want to ask what it is. Don't. The question you need to ask is: 'What part of you still believes the past is gone?'"

His pulse throbbed in his ears.

Leah's handwriting moved between poetry and precision, the way she used to speak when she was nervous but excited.

"It doesn't take you *back*, Aldous. Not exactly. It takes you *into* memory...the world's memory. The bones of the earth, the echoes inside stone, the silence in stained glass. Places where time folds, and belief becomes architecture. But it's dangerous. You won't just *see* the past. You'll feel it. You'll carry it. And it will try to carry you."

He looked up from the letter, heart pounding.

Outside the barn, the sky was the color of bruised ash. Clouds rolled like slow thunder.

He turned the machine over. There was no button, no screen. Just one small indentation in the center, like a thumbprint made in cooling glass.

He placed his thumb into it.

The machine didn't hum. It didn't glow.

It sighed.

The world flickered.

And then....

Silence.

Not the kind he knew.

This silence had gravity. It pulled at the skin, slowed his blood. The barn was gone. The field was gone. Even the wind had stopped whispering.

He stood in darkness, not black, but the kind of darkness that's full. Breathing. Listening back.

And then, slowly, the world began to reassemble.

He was in a city.

Ancient. Towering. Carved from white stone and lit by torches. The air smelled of blood and incense. Bells rang, not in celebration, but in warning. Priests walked with their heads lowered, clutching scrolls. Children recited verses like punishment.

He turned and saw it:

A temple being built.

Not just *any* temple. The *first* one. Massive, brutal, holy. Carved with precision meant to last longer than belief. It wasn't a place of peace. It was a place of power. Built not for God, but for men who *claimed* to speak for Him.

Aldous stepped forward.

His boots echoed.

No one saw him.

He wasn't there. Not fully. He was thought. He was wind. He was *witness*.

He drifted through the structure, past laborers breaking their backs, slaves dying beneath the weight of marble and doctrine. And above them, robed men scribbled rules. Wrote sins into law. Drew borders around what could be *questioned.*

His breath caught in his throat.

This was it.

Religion not as spirit—but as system.

A machine of control.

He saw scrolls forged, stories twisted, names erased. He saw myths born not from wonder, but from *strategy.* He saw fear being woven into prayer.

And somewhere deep inside, something in him cracked.

Not with anger.

But with a kind of grieving he didn't have language for.

Then the light shifted.

The temple aged in seconds. Stone wore down. Statues lost their faces. The gods changed names. The robes changed colors. But the *structure* remained.

Power recycled.

He saw crusades. Holy wars. Witch burnings. False prophets. Political sermons. Bombs blessed by sacred texts. People kneeling in pews while their questions were shot down like heresy.

He screamed.

But his voice made no sound.

Then everything collapsed inward.

The city folded like a dying flame.

And he was falling again.

He woke in the barn.

Gasping. Cold sweat. Blood on his nose.

The machine was dark beside him.

Leah's letter lay on his chest.

He wasn't the same.

He couldn't be.

He had seen it.....the birth of the lie. The first handshake between faith and fear. The roots of the myth that had cost him Leah. That had silenced minds like hers for centuries.

And he finally understood what she had meant when she said, *"You never really lose someone. You just meet them again in different questions."*

Because now, the questions were burning in him.

And they had faces.

And history.

And a voice.

His.

Chapter Five :

A Mirror at the End of Time

The barn was quiet, but not still.

Aldous lay on his side, curled around the machine like a child might hold a toy after a nightmare. The candle had burned out, the air smelled of soot and dry straw, and his breath felt heavier, like he'd returned from somewhere oxygen had never touched.

His body was here, but his mind was still inside that temple...inside that system.

He sat up slowly. His hand trembled as it brushed dried blood from under his nose.

He didn't cry.

He just sat there.

The birds outside had begun singing again, but they sounded far away. Like they belonged to a different world. Maybe they did.

He reached for Leah's letter. The edges were creased now, corners curled like they were retreating from something. He didn't read it again. He didn't need to. Her words were carved into him.

He stood, knees weak, and walked out into the morning.

The world looked normal.

That unsettled him more than anything else.

The sky was soft with clouds, golden light spilling across the hills. A stream bubbled nearby. Cows lowed in a distant field. A butterfly flitted across his path, unaware of gods and temples and how easy it is to bend truth into chains.

Aldous laughed. Not joy. Not despair.

Just disbelief.

"I went back," he whispered, as if saying it aloud might make it real. "I saw it. All of it."

He walked.

Not toward any town or path. Just forward, letting the ground decide.

As he moved, pieces of what he saw kept blooming in his memory like bruises.

The boy punished for asking if the stars had names before the priests gave them.

The girl burned because she claimed to hear the divine without needing a church.

The man who smiled as he signed a decree, knowing it would start a war in the name of a god he didn't believe in.

He stumbled on a rock and fell to his knees.

For a second, he didn't move.

Then he screamed, not with rage, but grief. Deep, cracked grief.

Because he realized something then.

This world he had returned to this quiet field, this morning sun, it hadn't changed. Only he had.

And now he didn't know how to live in it anymore.

Later that day, Aldous found a small roadside diner...half-abandoned, windows cracked, but still standing.

He walked in.

The bell above the door gave a dry clang.

An old man sat at the counter, reading a newspaper from five years ago. A woman behind the counter poured him coffee like she'd been doing it her whole life.

They looked up, saw Aldous, and nodded like he was just another traveler.

He sat.

"Long road?" the woman asked, wiping her hands on a faded cloth.

Aldous hesitated. Then nodded. "Yeah. Longer than I expected."

She smiled gently and poured him coffee.

"You look like you've seen something terrible."

He stared into the dark liquid. "I saw the beginning of a lie. And how far people will go to protect it."

The man turned a page. "History or religion?"

"Both."

The woman didn't flinch. "Same difference."

They sat in silence a while.

Then the old man spoke, not looking up. "So what now? You gonna save the world?"

Aldous laughed again, this time almost bitter. "I don't even know if I believe in the world anymore."

The woman leaned forward. "Then start smaller."

He looked up.

"Believe in the people who hurt," she said. "The ones who still ask questions. Who don't pray for power but for peace. Believe in them."

And somehow, it felt like Leah was in her voice. Just a little.

He nodded.

•

That night, Aldous camped under the stars. The machine lay beside him, inert now, like a weapon that had done its damage.

He stared up at the sky for hours.

Not praying.

Not hoping.

Just watching.

And he began to whisper- not to any god, not even to Leah.

Just to the universe.

"Why do we exist?" he asked. "To build stories that cage us? To hurt in the name of things we made up?"

No answer.

But there were stars.

So many stars.

He closed his eyes.

And then he spoke again.

"I don't know what's real anymore. But I know what felt real. The pain. The questions. Her voice. That has to be enough."

And somewhere in the dark, he felt it:

Not an answer.

But an understanding.

A kind of quiet that didn't silence him, but held him.

•

In the morning, he kept walking.

He met others.

A teacher who left the church to build a library. A soldier who refused to fire on villages after reading a banned poem. A child who painted gods with no faces, only hearts.

Each one carried their own scar, their own doubt.

But also something else.

Choice.

And Aldous listened.

He didn't try to fix anything. He wasn't a prophet. He wasn't chosen.

He was just a man who had seen the first lie and decided not to live by it.

•

Years passed.

He wrote sometimes. Leah's journal filled with ink, and his own beside it. Writings not of doctrine, but of feeling. Of doubt. Of moments that meant nothing and everything.

People began to share them.

They called it "The Quiet Fire."

He didn't ask for that.

He just kept writing.

Kept walking.

•

And then one day, he came to a cliff.

It overlooked a vast ocean, moonlight scattering like memory across the water.

He sat at the edge.

The machine was still in his bag.

He hadn't used it again.

But tonight, he held it one last time.

He didn't turn it on.

He didn't need to.

Because he finally understood:

"Time was not a line, or a circle. It was a wound. And a wound, once named, could begin to heal."

He left the machine there.

Let the tide take it.

And walked into the darkness.

Not to escape.

But to continue.

Because the journey was never about changing the past.

It was about refusing to repeat it.

And somewhere, far behind him, a voice like Leah's whispered..

"Keep asking."

The ocean swelled and breathed, as if taking the machine into its depths with reverence, not violence. Aldous didn't look back. He had said goodbye. To guilt. To grief. To the illusion of control.

But as his feet moved forward into the night, the air behind him shimmered.

A hum like memory being rewritten.

A portal opened- soft, glowing, stitched not with light but with *knowing*. The kind that made your skin ache with recognition before your mind could catch up.

And through it.....

Leah.

She stood barefoot on air. Smiling like she never left. Her presence didn't break the laws of nature. It *rewrote* them.

Aldous froze.

Time paused.

His chest caved with emotion too big for his ribs to hold.

He took one step. Then another. And she ran to him.

They collided like stars collapsing inward, grief turning to gravity, loss transforming into reunion.

"I waited," she whispered.

"I searched," he choked.

"I know."

He pressed his forehead to hers, trembling with the weight of everything unsaid. "You're real."

Leah's hand slid to his cheek. "As real as the questions that brought you here."

His tears fell into her palms.

"I thought death took you," he whispered.

"It didn't," she said. "Death doesn't take. It *shifts*. We don't die, Aldous. We just... travel. Like light. Like thought. From one dimension to the next."

He pulled her close and wept.

Not from sorrow this time.

But from relief.

From the unbearable beauty of still having her.

Of being allowed this one last page.

The portal stayed open.

And hand in hand, they stepped through.

Epilogue:

The Conversation Beyond Time

They sat under a tree that cast no shadow.

In a dimension between storylines.

In a silence that didn't feel empty, but full. pregnant with meaning.

Aldous lay in the grass, head in Leah's lap, eyes toward a sky that pulsed with memory. Galaxies spun like thoughts. Stars blinked like questions.

"You know," he said softly, "I used to wonder why we even exist."

Leah smiled and looked up with him. "Still wondering?"

He nodded. "Yeah. But it doesn't hurt as much now."

She ran her fingers through his hair. "Maybe that's the point. Not to know. Just to wonder, together."

Aldous breathed in. The air tasted like nostalgia.

He turned to face her.

"I was so afraid," he said. "Of dying. Of forgetting you. Of the world never changing."

She looked into his eyes. "You changed, Aldous. And that changed the world."

He broke. Quietly. Peacefully. The way a wave finally releases itself on the shore.

"I kept asking," he whispered. "Even when it hurt."

"I know," she said, tears lining her lashes. "I heard you. Every time."

He kissed her knuckles. "So this is what comes after?"

She nodded. "This, and everything else. We move. We meet. We ask better questions."

He grinned through the blur of tears. "And the answers?"

She shrugged gently. "Maybe love is the answer. Or maybe it's the question we're meant to never stop asking."

They sat in the light of stars that no longer existed, holding each other in a world where time no longer ticked. Where pain had memory, but not power.

Where everything they lost found them again.

And somewhere in the distance

Another version of Aldous opened a book.

Another version of Leah lit a candle.

And another story began.

THE END
(Or maybe, the next beginning.)

www.ingramcontent.com/pod-product-compliance
Lightning Source LLC
Chambersburg PA
CBHW062234150726

47991CB00006B/2579